Millie's Missing Yawn

PAVILION

Essex County Council

First published in the United Kingdom in 2018 by
Pavilion Children's Books
43 Great Ormond Street
London
WC1N 3HZ

An imprint of Pavilion Books Limited.

Publisher and Editor: Neil Dunnicliffe
Assistant Editor: Harriet Grylls
Art Director: Anna Lubecka

Text and Illustrations © You Jung Byun 2018

The moral rights of the author and illustrator have been asserted

ISBN: 9781843653844

A CIP catalogue record for this book is available from the British Library.

10 9 8 7 6 5 4 3 2 1

Reproduction by Mission Productions Ltd, Hong Kong

Printed by Toppan Leefung Ltd, China

This book can be ordered directly from the publisher online at www.pavilionbooks.com, or try your local bookshop.

One night Millie just couldn't get to sleep,
and she couldn't work out why.

She'd done everything she normally did before bed.

She'd taken a warm bath,

put on her favourite pyjamas,
brushed her teeth,

read her favourite book

and given her teddy Milo
a goodnight kiss.

The only thing Millie hadn't done was yawn a big, sleepy yawn...

"That's it! That's why I can't get to sleep.
I think I've lost my yawn!"

"Come on, Milo! We have to find my yawn so that
I can go to sleep and tomorrow can come."

First they saw Barley.

"Have you seen my yawn, Barley?"

"Sorry, no, I've been chasing Cucumber the cat all day and I'm very tired."

Woof-yawwwwnnn

"Oh, that's a shame. I'll carry on looking. Good night," said Millie.

Next Millie and Milo
saw Cucumber.

"Have you seen my
yawn, Cucumber?"

"No, sorry Millie, I've been
busy dodging Barley and
trying to catch Douglas.
I'm worn out."

Mee-yawwwwnnn

"Have *you* seen my
yawn, Douglas?"

"I wish I could help,
Millie, but I've been
looking for crumbs all day,
and avoiding Cucumber.
Now it's time for
me to sleep."

Coo-yawwwwnnn

No one
had seen
Millie's yawn
anywhere.

It looked like
she would have
to be even more
adventurous...

"Hello Lady Liberty, have you seen my yawn?"

"Sorry, Millie. I've had so many people
inside my head today, it's been very tiring."

Yawwwwnnn

"Dear Moai Heads, have you seen my yawn?"

"No, Millie. We've seen many, many things, but not your yawn."

Yawwwwnnn

"Hello Mona Lisa, have you seen my yawn?"

"No, sorry, Millie. I've been too busy smiling all day, and now I've got to..."

Yawwwwnnn

Poor Millie! She'd come so far, but no one had seen her yawn...

She wouldn't give up. "I must find my yawn! Come on, Milo."

"H-h-hello p-p-penguins.
Have any of you seen my yawn?"

"Oh no, sorry, we've been far too busy skiing
and sledging and making snowballs."

Yawwwwnnn

"Phew, it's really hot here. Have you seen my yawn, hippo?"
"No, I'm afraid not, Millie. But check out MY yawn!"

Yawwwwnnn

"Excuse me, Great Sphinx, but have you seen my yawn around here?"

"Sorry, Millie. I've been here for more than 4,000 years, but I haven't seen your yawn."

Yawwwwnnn

By now, Millie had been all over the world, and her yawn was *still* nowhere to be found.

It looked like they would have to go even further...

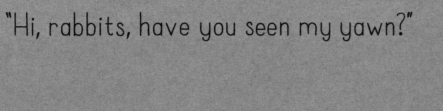

"Hi, rabbits, have you seen my yawn?"

"I'm afraid not, Millie. We've been too busy digging cheese for our party tomorrow."

Yawwwwnnn

Millie had been all the way to
the moon to look for her yawn,
but she still hadn't found it...

And so, at last: "Come on, Milo," Millie said.
"I give up. Let's go home."

Back home in bed, gazing up at the moon, Millie thought about all the friends she had met that night.

"What a...

big...

adventure...

we've had, Milo."

Yawwwwnnn!

After a great big yawn, Millie fell fast asleep.

Goodnight!